Saint Vitus' Dance

Saint Vitus' Dance

by Jill Rubalcaba

Clarion Books
New York

Clarion Books
a Houghton Mifflin Company imprint
215 Park Avenue South, New York, NY 10003
Copyright © 1996 by Jill Rubalcaba

Text is 13.5/17-point Garamond 3

For information about this and other Houghton Mifflin
trade and reference books and multimedia products,
visit The Bookstore at Houghton Mifflin on the World Wide Web
at (http://www.hmco.com/trade/).

Printed in the USA

Library of Congress Cataloging-in-Publication Data

Rubalcaba, Jill.
Saint Vitus' dance / by Jill Rubalcaba.
p.   cm.
Summary: Fourteen-year-old Melanie must come to terms with her mother's
incurable illness and the possibility that she herself may develop the disease.
ISBN 0-395-72768-5
[1. Huntington's chorea—Fiction.]   I. Title.
PZ7.R8276Sai   1996
[Fic]—dc20   96-1260
CIP
AC

BP   10 9 8 7 6 5 4 3 2 1

For Dan, because he's my buddy.

—*Smooch*

Chapter
1

$\mathcal{I}$ WAS THIRTEEN AND A HALF years old when
Mama started losing her mind to the sickness.
Maybe I would have caught on earlier had it
been summer, when our evenings on the porch
rockers followed the swoops of the bats, or even
fall, when Papa always teased Mama about turning the kitchen into a sauna with her nonstop
canning. But it was winter, and winters in
Cutter's Falls always lasted five weeks too long.

Folks started getting cranky toward the middle of March, when hints of spring were buried
in yet another ten inches of snow. Every March,
Bella Parks threw her husband Zeke's clothes
out the second floor bedroom window, half of
them catching in the branches of the cherry tree

below. He'd sleep in the choir loft at St. Monica's until she cooled off. "Cabin fever," people would say, hanging a windblown argyle sock on the Parkses' picket fence.

And every March our school's principal, Mr. Forsyth, would be missing the wishing well from his front lawn. It would show up the next morning. Last year it was hanging from the bell tower at the Episcopal church. "Cabin fever," people muttered, looking up.

All of Cutter's Falls was unsettled this time of year. So when the storekeeper at Howard's Market ran out of fresh dill and Mama told him to take a trip south—not to Florida, mind you, but the south every church-going Catholic bruises knees to stay out of—I ducked behind the display of potato chips, thankful Mama was just pitching a fit over some spice and not giving up Papa's BVDs to the wind.

Standing behind the chips, I could feel my face blotchy red from the prickling embarrassment my mama's tirade was bringing me. Even though I knew somewhere deep down that things weren't right, that Mama would never make a scene over something as silly as dill, I still laughed behind my hand when Mrs. Winslow winked and mouthed the words "Cabin fever" while wiping her hands on her butcher's apron.

Our cats had grown lazy and petulant staying inside long nights. Old Sage spent his days in the bay window stretched out in the sun, but today even the young ones, Bailey and Scribbles, were sprawled about the kitchen in the patches of late afternoon sun, soaking up the warmth and the smell of bacon fat. They gave indifferent audience to Mama's lecturing on the Japanese having control of the dill industry. They followed her with their eyes from the stove to the sink to the electric frying pan sitting on the counter, until like a windup car she ran down and out of complaints. Then those cats nestled their outstretched chins back between their front paws and yawned at her frenzy.

I swiped a meatball from the frying pan while Mama was turned to the sink. It wasn't as tasty without the dill, but I wasn't about to say a word on that subject. I feared she'd start in ranting and raving again about the state of produce in this nation, clanging on the side of the soup kettle with her wooden spoon.

"Melanie Genzler, quit sampling and go wash up, then set the table. Your papa will be getting home from the mill shortly. He's been so tired lately, I want dinner waiting on him so's he can turn in early tonight."

I was folding the napkins when Papa trudged into the mudroom. He sat down heavily on the deacon's bench, unlaced his work boots, and placed them side by side next to the radiator before he said, "Evenin'."

"How are my two favorite ladies tonight?" Papa asked the same question every night, accompanied by a peck on the top of my head and a big kiss for Mama. You could generally tell how his day had gone by the playfulness in his voice. Tonight he sounded bone tired. He lifted the soup kettle's lid, breathing deep the aroma the steam offered up.

"Lil, you spoil a man. Fellas at the mill complain of casserole dishes with notes taped to the cover greeting them when they get home. Homemade soup. Smells real fine."

Mama was at the sideboard, arranging the condiments. I said a quick prayer that she wouldn't start in on the dill. I was in such a state that "Now I lay me down to sleep" was all that came to mind. I knew it wasn't right for the occasion, but I was hoping God would understand. He must have, on account of Mama turned with the platter of meatballs and a smile plastered on her face.

"Howie Jenkins's boy quit the mill today," Papa said, tucking his napkin into the collar of his shirt. "That's the third one this month run off to Clewiston."

"Now, George, it's the same every spring, don't go blaming it on Howie's son. The big city fills a boy's head with cotton candy willies. It can't be helped." Mama scooped more meatballs onto Papa's plate. "Howie is probably fit to be tied. You know he'd never leave you short if there was something he could do about it."

"Well maybe so, but this means I'll be working late until we get someone to replace them or we'll fall behind on the orders. I can't afford to give my customers reason to go looking elsewheres. Not in this economy."

Papa took a bite of meatball, never noticing the lack of dill. "When my daddy first started this business, it was just him and Ma and the one hired man. Sometimes I wonder what he'd say if he could see it now."

"He'd be so proud, he'd be busting britches buttons." Mama smoothed Papa's fork-holding hand. "He loved the mill."

"He loved you too, Lil."

Mama got all flustered like she always does when Papa pays her a compliment. She smoothed the napkin in her lap, *tsk*ing out denials, but the sparkle in her eyes betrayed her pleasure. Papa missed it. You could tell he was still thinking on work.

The mill stood in a long line of brick factories built right to the edge of the road with a cobblestone sidewalk barely wide enough for a man to walk a dog along. Every year another factory fell out of business and Papa bought the building. I think Papa bought them because he couldn't stand the sight of them standing empty. Now Papa owns the whole block, and the mill employs half the town of Cutter's Falls. Not that that is so many people, Cutter's Falls being so small you could spit across it. Still, with every new building Papa's hours get longer. It's been a long time since Papa surprised Mama and me by coming home in the middle of the afternoon to take us to the matinee in Clewiston.

"Good dinner as always, Lil." He smiled at Mama. Mama held a cold forgotten meatball skewered to her fork. It hovered halfway between her mouth and the plate.

"I made them without dill. The market—"

I jumped up, tipping my chair over backward, scraping plates furiously, and stacking them with a clatter. "Big test tomorrow. I really should start studying."

"Well now, it's a pleasure to see you so eager to be getting on with your homework." Papa flicked the newspaper to reverse the crease and lost himself in the business section.

Mama set the meatball down.

The cats came weaving around chair legs to investigate the possibility of table scraps.

Mama looked a bit feverish. Maybe I was coming down with something too. I felt so tired all the time.

When all the dishes were piled in the drying rack, I took a good look at Mama bent over the mending. She looked all right, the dill forgotten.

I didn't really have a test the next day, but I did have a reading assignment for history. On page thirty-one I must have dozed off. When I startled awake, the quiet surprised me. Took me a moment to locate myself. My dream had been loud. Real loud. I'd been baby-sitting for dozens of babies, who were all crying. I didn't know which one to go to first, so I just sat down in the middle of it all and cried right along with them.

Now I used my index fingers like windshield wipers to clear the tears from my cheeks, turned out my desk lamp, and crawled between my flannel sheets. Bailey and Scribbles were curled up in a pile at the foot of my bed, so I couldn't straighten out my legs without putting them off. I fell asleep all tucked up tight, dreaming about fields of dill surrounded by barbed wire with a Japanese guard at each corner. Instead of rifles they shouldered huge wooden spoons, and on their heads were soup kettles that they clanged with regularity.

Chapter 2

"YOU PROMISED, PAPA!" The wailing in my voice was embarrassing, but I just couldn't help it. He'd forgotten. Forgotten the most important night in my life. My first school dance.

I'd waited. Waited on the deacon's bench with my ankles crossed and swinging, like entwined dancers racing back and forth across a ballroom floor. My new patent leather shoes caught the light just so. The sparkle was like a lightning flash. Flash. Swing. Flash. Swing. I counted three thousand four hundred flashes before I moved to the kitchen to keep an eye on the clock.

Mama'd gone to bed with one of her "funny heads." If only she'd learned to drive, I wouldn't have been waiting on Papa. I planned on taking my driver's test the day of my sixteenth birthday. Not a day later.

The dance started at seven o'clock. I was supposed to be meeting Marcy Davis at a quarter to seven in the girls' room behind the gym. Papa was to drive me. Only he forgot.

The pickup's lights swept the front porch at ten past eight. Too late to go. Everyone would be dancing and grouped off. How was I to walk in alone then? Papa looked so sorry, I should've let it rest. But I couldn't. I'd waited too long, I'd worked myself up. I wanted him to be hurting the way I was.

"You just don't care about us anymore. You only care about the mill." I knew that wasn't true, but I knew saying it would hurt. Hurt him bad. And that's what I wanted right then. When I saw his face crumple, I wasn't so sure anymore. It didn't give me the satisfaction I was hoping for. Only I couldn't stop. It was like I was running downhill out of control. "I'll never forgive you." He looked sorrier than Marcy Davis's old hound dog after getting caught rooting through the garbage. I didn't know eyes could droop so.

I don't know what came over me. I couldn't

help it. I just burst into tears. I could barely see him through the haze the water in my eyes created. I couldn't hold it. Those tears just spilled out all over the place no matter how hard I stomped around the kitchen trying to force them to stop coming.

He grabbed me by the shoulders and pulled me into one of his bear hugs. His chin rested on the top of my head, and he said, "Tomorrow's Saturday. It'd be a good day to go feeding a sweet tooth. Anyone in this kitchen have such a thing?"

He was trying to make up. Deep inside I wanted to say something nice to soothe his sorrows, but the rest of me wasn't cooperating. I pulled away.

He stuffed a dollar in my hand. I wouldn't open my fist, wouldn't give him the satisfaction. The bill got all wadded up in the struggle. He poked it between my clenched fingers.

"Tomorrow you trot yourself down to May Parker's general store and get yourself a sack full of penny candy."

I think he wanted to hug me again, but I wouldn't look him in the eye. So he stood, his arms dangling awkwardly by his sides.

I never so much as said thank you for the dollar, just spun on my heels and swam through the blur of tears to my bedroom.

I rubbed the shine back into my patent leathers with the corner of my bedspread before wrapping them again in tissue paper. I put them in the shoe box and onto the top shelf of my closet. I pushed the box way back to where it wouldn't be looking at me and went to bed thinking of Marcy still waiting in the girls' room.

Chapter
3

_I_ SKIPPED ALL THE WAY to Parker's general store, kicking up dirt and sending stones flying down Dunn's Lane. I'd talked to Marcy early this morning in whispered tones while sitting under the telephone table's long skirt so as not to wake Mama. Papa was already at the mill.

Marcy said the dance was awful. Worse than awful, a disaster. She demanded to know how I knew not to show up. Was I in telepathic communication with the popular group? All the cheerleaders—and the football, basketball, and soccer teams—had stayed home, and only the dweebs had gone. She was mortified. By now everyone knew who had gone and who hadn't. The lines were drawn. Why hadn't I told her?

My not going had set me apart with the popular ones, or at least not thrown me in with the
others. Now I felt even worse about letting Papa
go on hurting. But I knew I'd never tell him.
Not that he'd take the dollar back. I'd just gone
too far to make amends. Best to pretend nothing
had happened.

When I got just shy of Rosilda Lamour's house,
I crossed the street. Miss Rosilda's a psychic.
Mama says fortune-telling is a load of nonsense,
but once her bridge club got their palms read for
a lark. When Mama's turn came, Miss Rosilda
took hold of Mama's hands. Miss Rosilda's eyes
rolled back in her head like she was coming on
to a faint, but she snapped to right fast and
shoved Mama out of her house, crossing herself
with one hand and pushing Mama with the
other. It scared Mama silly until Papa took to
calling her his little she-devil and teased her out
of her nervous spell.

I wished he'd take the time to see the nervous
spell she was in now. She was so jumpy, she was
dropping everything, then scrambling to clean
it up before Papa noticed. Yesterday morning I'd
found her on her knees crying over Grandma

Darling Heart's cut-glass vase shattered all around her. I backed out of the room before she saw me and left her to her weeping.

I walked the sidewalk in front of Miss Rosilda's house, not studying the cracks in the sidewalk at all but trying to peer behind the lace curtains that hung in her parlor window. Rumor had it that she had a crystal ball sitting in the middle of the front room.

Mayor Baldwin's wife came out the side door of Miss Rosilda's. She was in a house-afire hurry to latch the garden gate and be on her way. She looked both ways before emerging from the cover of the side hedge. No one in town admitted to frequenting Miss Rosilda's. When Mrs. Baldwin's scarf snagged on the fence post, she yanked at it, ripping it rather than taking the time to untangle it. *Wait until I tell Marcy. The mayor's wife, of all people.*

. . .

The glass case alongside the cash register at Parker's general store is full of penny candy: jawbreakers, buttons on paper strips, red hots, jujubes, wax lips, and such. Stenciled on the glass in black lettering outlined in gold is the word CONFECTIONS. Most things are more than a penny, but a dollar will still get you a small brown bag full. I squatted down, pressing my forehead and hands to the cool glass, trying to make up my mind. Was I in a chocolate kiss kind of mood or a red licorice one?

Miss Kramer, the librarian, and Mrs. Barton, who runs the boardinghouse across the street, were by the dairy coolers. They must not have seen me come in. They couldn't see me now, squatting down low. They were talking freely as you please about Mama.

"Emma Bickman sat behind her in church and said she had no undergarments on." Mrs. Barton's nasally twang made the word "undergarments" sound soiled.

"Bella said she tried to send the electric bill without a stamp."

"It's early, but there's no question it's 'the change.'"

"Esther went through 'the change' at thirty-six. Lil's not so young."

I could feel the tips of my ears burning. I knew they must be beet red with the thought of

Mama at church stark naked under her dress. How could she do this to me?

Forgetting the dollar in my pocket, forgetting the penny candy, I bolted like a jackrabbit, slamming into the glass door so hard, I thought my arm might go straight through. The silver bell hanging on a length of twine over the door to announce the comings and goings of May Parker's customers set to clanging like I'd tripped the alarm at the firehouse. The frenzied ringing followed me past the old oak trees draping Dunn's Lane.

I ran home pumping my arms and stretching my legs till my whole body was crying in a pain fiercer than the one in my heart. I didn't stop then, didn't stop until my lungs felt like exploding because I couldn't get enough oxygen no matter how much and how hard I sucked air in. Then I slowed down and tried not to think of anything at all. Tried to empty my brain right out on the cracked pavement.

The black earth was heaving and rutted from the freeze and thaw of early spring. Little puddles, frozen over, filled the furrows. I stomped them, shattering the membrane of ice.

"The change" kept rattling around in my

empty skull. Things were changing all right. The whole town could see that. Everyone could see that—everyone except Papa.

I was just across from Miss Rosilda's place. I wondered what she could see in that crystal ball of hers.

Chapter 4

AT SUPPER PAPA BENT OVER his plate. He was so preoccupied with the overload at the mill, he wasn't seeing a thing out of the ordinary.

Mama spooned turnip onto Papa's plate. Her hand shook so, she was in danger of missing the plate altogether. How could Papa not see? I'd come to reason it would take a serving of turnip in his lap to get him to take notice.

I tried sending a mental message to Papa. I concentrated real hard. I willed him to look at Mama's hand.

Look at her. Really look at her.

I clenched my teeth till my jaw ached and focused every particle, every atom, of my being into that message.

Look at her. Really look at her.

Mama hid her hands in her lap, twisting her napkin. Her dinner lay untouched on her plate. I hadn't seen her eat in days now. I wondered if she ate during her prowling hours before dawn. That's when she and the cats stalked back and forth between the refrigerator and the glass slider that opens onto the porch.

A week earlier I had snuck downstairs and found them pacing. Back and forth. Back and forth. Not even slowing at the turns. Just charging full ahead like they'd walk right on up the wall but instead turning on a pinhead at the last second. Back and forth. Back and forth. I snuck down three nights running to see if there'd be some change in route. After that I just listened to the scuffling from my bed.

My eyes narrowed trying to burn the message through Papa's skull. I tried shooting rays from my eyeballs into his.

Look at her. Really look at her.

"Good dinner as always, Lil." Papa dabbed at his mouth with his napkin. "I'll take my coffee in the den. I've got paperwork." Papa carried two briefcases home most nights now. One had broken open from the strain of overstuffing. He kept the bulging case tied shut with clothesline.

We all used to take a walk evenings after supper. I'd walk on ahead, taking comfort in the gentle rise and fall of conversation following me. I liked to stay far enough ahead so I couldn't make out the words, but not so far I couldn't hear Mama's tinkling laughter and the hum of Papa's mellow voice. It reminded me of falling asleep in the backseat of the car on the way to the lake house weekends when I was little. Listening to their voices in my half sleep. But we hadn't taken a stroll in months, and Papa said we'd be late opening the lake house this year. And Mama was getting more peculiar every day.

Papa filled his mug from the coffeepot perking on the stove and took it to his desk in the den. He hadn't stopped fidgeting into place before Sage jumped into his lap and curled up for a nap. Papa stroked the old tom's head while he worked his way through the stack of files.

Mama put her hand on my arm, but I jumped back like I'd connected with the wrong end of a cattle prod. Maybe she'd intercepted the brain waves I was sending Papa over dinner.

I turned my back on her, not wanting to see the look in her eyes. What could I do? Why was she tormenting me with that look? Papa was the grown-up here. Papa was the one she should be dogging after. It wasn't my responsibility.

She didn't push. Just left me to the dishes. But every now and then she'd look over to where I was scouring pots and shake her head. I scrubbed those pots past the crusty remains of dinner, past the brown spots left from days before, past the gray aluminum to the raw shiny metal below.

. . .

I started going to church an extra day a week to pray for Mama. Didn't let my mind stray through the entire Rosary. I figured if I could get the whole way to the end without so much as one unrelated thought, that meant He would help Mama.

I tried to come up with a promise good enough to make it tempting. Like *I'll pray every day on my hands and knees for the rest of my life if only . . .* or *I'll spread the word of God every chance I get forevermore if only . . .* But it was hard to come up with a deal that would tempt Him when the devil had failed, and I imagined the devil's deals were a whole lot finer than mine. So I stuck to trying to prove how earnest I was by being as holy as I could possibly be while saying my Our Fathers. If things got worse, I could always escalate.

Mama was scaring me with her muttering and jerking. She'd twist her hands in her apron and talk over the top of my head. She'd quote scripture about cleanliness but most days never got around to combing her own hair. It got so I didn't know if I was walking the extra two miles to church to save Mama or to avoid her.

There was no hiding her queer behavior any longer. I think even Papa was starting to notice that something wasn't right. Though he hadn't admitted it to himself yet. He still talked up what a lucky man he was and brought her tea in bed every morning like always. Only now after his shower he'd bring the cold, untouched tea back downstairs and dump it down the sink.

I never asked Marcy over after school anymore. She pretended nothing was the matter, but with the subject hanging so heavy in the air between us and me not wanting to talk about it and her knowing that, it was hard to think of other things to say. Anything we could think of to talk about seemed insignificant compared to what we weren't saying. So when the silences started outdistancing the conversation, we started pretending we didn't see each other when we passed in the corridors at school.

I knew tongues were wagging around Cutter's Falls. I knew the talk would more than likely make my ears curl. It was hard to ignore some of the getups Mama did the marketing in. Wednesday she'd worn Aunt Katha's rhinestone brooch pinned dead center to a coonskin cap I'd worn in my second-grade play. She had the cap perched on backward. When the tail dangled down in her face, she just tucked it behind her left ear.

On top of that her walk had grown unsteady. She walked like a toddler playing dress-up in her mama's high heels. And she slurred her words or sputtered them. You'd think hearing those strange sounds falling from her lips would silence her, but it did just the opposite. She carried on a steady stream of conversation, mumbling to herself, then raising her voice when folks were nearby as if she'd been talking to them all along.

The only time she acted near normal was when she was around Papa. You could see her straining from the effort. The cords in her neck stretched so taut, they looked near snapping, and she kept her hands shoved deep in her pockets when they weren't busy with some chore. Her charade wasn't near good enough to fool the cats, but it did the job on Papa.

Grandma Darling Heart always said a hog sees only the slops in the sallow, meaning folks see just what they've a mind to see. Where Papa's mind was at only the good Lord knew, although I'd taken to praying for it to show up, seeing that my efforts on Mama weren't getting through.

Chapter
5

$\mathcal{I}$T WAS AT CHURCH that Marcy and I patched things up. I was saying the Rosary. I'd made it to the third decade of the Glorious Mysteries without one stray thought and was feeling optimistic. Marcy came to my pew and slid in without genuflecting. Marcy was always sitting when she should be kneeling and kneeling when she should be standing. She never could concentrate enough to get it right. So I wasn't surprised that she forgot her holy obligation.

"Melanie."

I bowed my head into my fistful of beads. I was in a fix now. If I spoke to her, I'd mess up and all the praying I'd done so far would be for nothing. But if I ignored her, I'd miss out on what might be my last chance to make things right with her. Marcy and I had shared everything for as far back as I could remember, and I was missing her company fiercely.

There was something warming about Marcy Davis, like putting on flannel pajamas right out of the dryer. Maybe best friends are like that.

"How's your mother?" By that very question I could see Marcy wasn't going to let something heavy lie between us anymore. I knew it was up to me now. I could say, "Just fine, thank you," and we'd both know the friendship couldn't bear the load. She'd probably spent quite some time thinking on how to handle this so we could both walk away unhurt.

I figured I needed our friendship more now than ever, so I said, "Not too good. She's looking like a robot that's got a short in her wiring."

Marcy just nodded and took my hand and squeezed it. I could tell she was smiling away tears. I was doing the same. It felt good to have Marcy back.

"I've got to go," she whispered, looking over to where her mother was waiting in the back of the church. "But I'll call you tonight."

When she left, it was like the sun had gone behind a cloud. The air felt cold again.

Oh Mama, what's wrong with you? I realized I was shivering. I'd been shivering since I'd found her sketch pad. Mama was never without her sketch pad. That is until recently. I'd be studying or watching TV when all of a sudden I'd feel the hairs on the back of my neck prickle and there she'd be, that little frown of concentration puckering her brow, her hand skating the charcoal all over the page. She even had a drawing of Papa on the toilet until he made her rip it up when he found Marcy and me giggling out of control over her sketch pad one afternoon. It was the only time I've ever seen Papa embarrassed. The tips of his ears looked like the blood had come to the outside.

Yesterday I'd gone to the attic to put some of my heavier sweaters in the cedar chest until next winter, and I found Mama's sketch pad. I sat on the trunk and began flipping through it. Smiling at first at the scenes: our orange tom, Sage, under the bird feeder; Papa and me playing chess; Papa fly fishing. But halfway through the book things started to go wrong. The pictures kept getting darker, like she was pressing harder and harder on the charcoal pencil. There'd be places where I could tell she'd pressed so hard the pencil broke, leaving a big black mark.

Toward the end I couldn't even make out what she was drawing. Just black lines jutting out at odd angles. The last few drawings, if you could call them that, were a nightmare of lines, as though she'd scratched back and forth over and over until the charcoal wore down and the wood tore at the paper.

It had scared me so, I'd thrown the book away from me like it had burned my flesh and run down the attic stairs. I knew if I was going to save Mama now, it was going to take the rest of my days on the glowing side of stained glass.

Chapter
6

———

SCRIBBLES WOKE ME with her pawing at the covers to be let under. I lifted the quilt, and she laid claim to the warm spot, forcing me to scoot over onto cold sheet while she purred and kneaded me awake.

It must have been a new moon, because I couldn't see my hand in front of my face, it was so dark. I lay there listening to the cedar tree outside my window scratching the aluminum siding.

At first I thought water was bubbling in the pipes, but when that gurgling noise came a second time, I felt sure it was coming from downstairs. I slipped out of bed and knotted my housecoat while stepping over the second stair on account of it squeaks.

If you lie on your belly on the landing, you

can see into the den between the bars of the stair railing. I was glad I was lying down for the sight I was to see.

Papa was bent over the photo album, his head buried in his hands. His shoulders were heaving. He was silent except for every now and then when a choking sob escaped.

I slid back into bed and waited until I heard Papa come up the stairs. His step was slow and heavy, like he was wearing lead boots. While he was in the bathroom washing up for bed, I slipped downstairs.

The photo album lay open on the coffee table. I moved his reading glasses off the page. I put the television on with no sound, and by the low, flickering light I studied the snapshots.

They had been taken last summer at the lake house. There was one of Mama looking like a young girl. She was tanned and barefoot with her checkered blouse tied up in front. She was holding a fishing line shingled with perch. She was holding it as far away from her as she could get it. Her nose was wrinkled up and her body pulling away from the dangling fish as if they'd jump off the line and get her.

She was laughing at Papa taking the picture,

and her mouth was puckered like she was in the midst of squealing "George." Which she was, because I remember as soon as Papa snapped the picture, she dropped the line and chased him clear around the boathouse. They were behind there for a spell squealing like a hungry litter of piglets. They were making such a racket, I began looking around to make sure we were alone on our finger of the lake.

Papa came back with her flung over his shoulder. She was pounding his back with her fists and both of them were laughing far too loud for their age. I dove into the water so I couldn't hear them making fools of themselves.

Sure would like to hear it now.

Chapter
7

I PRETENDED TO BE FASCINATED by the
mason jar filled with pickled beets, rolling it
around in my hand, watching the globes float,
suspended in the bloody syrup. But all the while
I kept my eye on Mama.

Mama's cart blocked the cereal aisle in
Howard's Market. She studied the ingredients
listed on the spine of the cornflakes box. She was
talking to the box, flicking her head from side to
side in short quick spasms.

She reminded me of the lizard Marcy gave me
for my tenth birthday. I kept him in an aquar-
ium tank until he escaped. He'd look at you
with that tilting head just like Mama was doing
to the cereal box. I suspect both made about the

same amount of sense. We found the lizard behind the couch during spring cleaning, all dried up.

Mama nodded in agreement with the box. I was hanging back, not wanting folks to think I was with her. I don't know who I thought I was fooling, this being a town where everyone either knows you or knows someone who does.

I turned the jar upside down and watched the beets bump to the surface. A little girl in a smocked calico dress, Mary Janes, and short white socks edged in lace stood between me and Mama. She had her thumb stuck into her cheek while she studied Mama conversing with the cornflakes.

She was one of Rhoda Lerner's little ones. Gabrielle or Annette, I couldn't keep track, Rhoda kept having them so fast.

When Rhoda steered her cart around the display pyramid of canned creamed corn, the little one pointed at Mama and said, "Look Mommy, zat da crazy lady you was talking to Miz Hepsie 'bout?"

"Hush, Gabrielle, mind your manners, it's not polite to stare." Rhoda nearly yanked Gabrielle's arm out of the socket, lifting her off her feet, and retreated back around the creamed corn. Her face was redder than the beets I was holding. I imagine mine was near the same.

When I was no bigger than Gabrielle, one of Papa's workers at the mill had gone and caught an arm in one of the looms. It had been mangled pretty bad. Papa took Mama and me to the hospital in Clewiston to wait alongside the man's family while the surgeon fixed him up. Papa paced while Mama hugged the wife, rocking her the way she did me when I was hurting.

In that waiting room there was a lady in a wheelchair. I'd never seen a wheelchair before and I was taken up with it. I couldn't keep my eyes off the lady.

Papa tried to distract me by reading from dog-eared magazines spilling off the end tables, but I'd have none of it. Mama said, "Now, George, let her look. Let her keep looking till she sees beyond the chair to the lady sitting in it."

I didn't understand her meaning then. I don't think I had till just now. Rhoda's flustered escape was far worse than little Gabrielle's wondering stare.

I started feeling pretty shameful about the way I'd been behaving. When I was sick, Mama never left my bedside. Reading to me until her voice grew hoarse, wringing facecloths in the washbasin to cool my forehead, and fussing with the covers and pillows so that sometimes I'd pretend to feel bad a little longer than I really did just to have her making so much of me. I think she knew that, too. I could tell because the worried look always left her face the same time the fever left my body, but she'd go on fussing until staying in bed became too high a price to pay for her attentions.

I put the beets back on the shelf and started toward Mama and her cereal friend.

Poor Mama. I hadn't touched her in weeks. Hadn't kissed her good night, hadn't put my arm around her. She was my mama after all, crazy or not. It was time I stopped holding out on her. Time I gave her some comfort.

I was halfway down the aisle when I heard it. Sounded like water falling onto a flat rock. I stopped, puzzled by the sound. It was coming from Mama. I looked in horror as the yellow puddle grew on the floor between her legs. Her cotton slacks darkened in blooming circles. My God, she was urinating right in the middle of Howard's Market. She hadn't even paused in her conversation with the cornflakes.

I was wishing Cutter's Falls would have its first-ever earthquake. That the floor right here beneath my feet would just split wide open and swallow me whole. I was torn between falling to my knees and praying for Armageddon and running as fast as my feet would take me.

I hadn't made up my mind which it would be when Papa came around the canned corn. He stopped, took in the situation with one grim look, and dragged me by the upper arm over to where Mama stood straddling the puddle. He put an arm around Mama's waist and sweet-talked her right out of Howard's Market, leaving the puddle of urine and Mama's half-loaded grocery cart behind. I followed in the wake of Papa's murmurings and watched him guide her home, an arm draped over her shoulders. I never even wondered what brought Papa to Howard's Market in the middle of a workday until later that evening Papa's assistant called him, and when I answered the phone, he asked how I'd liked the matinee in Clewiston. Guess this time we surprised Papa instead of the other way around.

We were halfway down Dunn's Lane before I noticed, clutched in Mama's arm, the box of cornflakes.

With each step the hate in me festered. Each step drove the demon spike deeper. Why me? Why *my* mama? The telephone lines in Cutter's Falls would be buzzing now, for sure.

I hate her, I hate her, I hate her, I wish she were dead.

Chapter
8

*T*HAT SAME NIGHT from my bed I heard Mama squeak the second step on her way to her nightly pacing. Not long after, the step squeaked again. Papa was going down after her.

I followed them. I stepped over the squeaking step and sat myself down on the landing. I stretched my nightgown over my knees and tucked it under my feet, breathing warm air into the neckhole.

The voices started as whispers. I couldn't make out much, but I knew by the tone Papa was wheedling her, trying to convince her of something she had no mind for. It wasn't long at all before the whispers got louder, like someone was gradually turning up the volume on the stereo, and shortly I had no trouble hearing what they had to say. I'd never heard them argue before. Whenever Papa was out of sorts, Mama'd surprise him with his favorite supper or have his slippers ready and a fire laid. When Mama got the blues, Papa'd tease her into better spirits or plan a grand evening taking her dancing. Mama loved to dance. They never before had been on the bad side at the same time.

"I've torn this house apart, Lil, and I can't find the bottle anywheres. You got to be telling me where you're hiding it."

"Did you hear that, George? I heard something."

"Your daddy was an alcoholic, Lil. You've got to face up to that. Sometimes the urge is more than a person can handle. It's not your fault, Lil, but you need help. You have to admit that much. You need help."

Scribbles leaped up the stairs. She sat on the squeaky step, a hind leg jutting out for a good cleaning. She took a few passes with her tongue, then stopped to listen, her ears drawn back, her leg straight out, forgotten for the moment.

"It's Father Mosley come calling."

"It's the middle of the night, for God's sake, Lil." Papa sounded tired.

Scribbles listened to the unfamiliar tones rising up the stairwell, then returned her full attention to her toilette, ignoring the argument with the contemptuous disregard that is a cat's God-given gift.

I focused on the cat, the voices downstairs rising and falling like swells on the sea. *Tomorrow I think maybe I'll wear my hair braided down the back, and when I get home I think maybe I'll start that journal I've been meaning to.* Marcy told me Mr. Emery was an alcoholic. He always smelled of whiskey and cigar smoke no matter how many mint leaves he tucked into his cheek. Mama never smelled like that. She smelled of witch hazel and rose petals.

"Pack up your things, Lil. I'm taking you over the ridge."

I knew where Papa was taking her. Most of the kids at school had some relative who'd been over the ridge to the sanatorium at one time or another. A few months of drying out, then they'd come back and everyone would treat them like the communion wafer. Gingerly at first for fear of breaking; then, once it dissolves, forgetting.

Some stayed out of the bottle, some moved on, a few went back over the ridge for another try at sobering up. Granddaddy up and disappeared when it looked like they'd be taking him back. No one knows where he took off to. Mama wouldn't hear a word about her daddy and the drink, so she made up stories of him off to seek his fortune.

. . .

The next morning I came down to a cold kitchen. The heat was still turned back. A piece of white paper was laid out on the kitchen table, a jelly jar holding it in place by the corner: "Grandma Darling Heart was taken ill, nothing serious, but your mama's going to her. I'll be bringing her to the station, then going to the mill. Will be home for supper."

I took a match from above the stove and burned the note over the sink.

Chapter
9

$\mathscr{A}$FTER ALL THE WAITING for spring to come, it blew in overnight. The pussywillows were the first to arrive. I picked the heads off, enough to fill my deep parka pockets to the point of bulging. I'd walk to and from school diving my hands into my pockets and rolling the furry balls in and out between my fingers.

Then the crocuses popped up all over the place, their purple petals and green leaves smearing the white blanket of snow like one of those impressionist painters dabbing on a clean canvas.

When the winds brought warm air thick with the smell of new greens being born, and the crocuses shriveled, the tulips began nodding their velvety heads. They were Mama's favorite. She had three tulip beds, sprinkled with daffodils. She'd cut a half dozen blossoms every day for the crystal vase that graced her dressing table.

The rest of the house was perfumed with lilac. No horizontal surface was safe from her arrangements. Papa was always teasing Mama that the house smelled like a funeral parlor. He'd grumble about it like a bear forced out of hibernating a month too soon, winking at me when Mama wasn't looking.

The lilac tree grew outside my room. With Mama gone, I'd open the window evenings and breathe deep the lilac and imagine her downstairs arranging purple blossoms into anything she could lay her hands on that held water: pickle jars, coffee cans, even Papa's green rubber boot once. At least until he noticed it sprouting lilacs on the sideboard and howled, "You've gone too far this time, Lil. When a man's boots are in jeopardy it's time to stop."

I knew from Marcy, whose uncle Bernie had gone to the sanatorium last summer, that it was customary for a drying-out period to last three months or more. It had been just three weeks when the news came from the sanatorium that they wanted to run a few tests. I had taken to picking up the phone upstairs, covering the mouthpiece so my breathing wouldn't give me away. They kept saying it was probably nothing, nothing at all, but it was best to be sure. They never did say what it was they wanted to be sure of, and just the way they said it made Papa unwilling to ask. So we waited. Waited for them to be sure.

I'd been trudging to church every day since Mama left, not wanting to go home and wander from room to room rattling about the house until Papa finished work. Once Papa did come home, we never quite knew what to say to each other. He'd tease me about having to dig out Granddaddy's old flintlock when the boys started to come calling, or how it was fine this being the first spring my knees weren't wearing a badge of scabs from falling off my bicycle a couple of times a week, but his heart wasn't in it. He'd ask me about my day, but for the life of me I couldn't think of a thing to tell him.

Except for the day our history teacher, Miss Olebar, disturbed a mud wasp nest when she opened the shutter for the first time that spring. Those wasps swarmed her faster than a leaf caught in a whirlwind. She ran out of the room, arms windmilling, fogged over by a cloud of angry mud wasps taking revenge.

The whole class froze, digesting the situation. Her screaming echoed back down the corridor into our classroom, where we sat as motionless as the statue of Abraham Lincoln overlooking the town green. Then we burst into laughter, which didn't stop even after the principal came down to cover the class. Mr. Forsyth lectured us on our insensitivity, but that just seemed to trigger more giggling.

I started to tell Papa about it, sitting there in the kitchen across the table from him. But Miss Olebar's flailing arms started me thinking of Mama and her twitchings. I stopped the tale smack in the middle of a sentence. I guess Papa knew where my thoughts had taken me, because he didn't try to prod me on with the telling. He avoided looking at me for the rest of supper. When I'd sneak a peek at him, he appeared older with every look. As if a fine gray powder were accumulating over his skin.

We ate out of cans mostly, neither of us know-ing how to cook or caring to try. We both liked beans, so that's what we ate. What they say about beans must be true, because the house didn't smell like lilacs, that's for sure.

Chapter
10

MARCY TOOK TO WALKING with me afternoons to church. On nice days she'd wait for me on the bench by the cement Mary in the blue bathtub. If it was raining, she'd spread her homework out on the pew behind me, working her pencil while I worked my prayers.

Standing on the granite step just outside the church doors, I had to squint through the blazing sun floating just over the tops of the sugar maples. Behind Marcy the sugaring buckets hung in clusters, forgotten, empty and clanging in the breeze.

"How'd it go today?" Marcy asked.

I sighed. "I can't seem to keep my mind from wandering. Being holy is tougher than it looks."

"Maybe if you went on one of those retreats where they don't eat anything but goat cheese and mineral water, or take a vow of poverty and wear nothing but cleaning rags." Marcy has what Miss Olebar calls "a dramatic flair." Every year she gets the lead in the class play. And as if that wasn't enough, she makes me act out every book she reads. At least she did until the Nancy Drew incident. Police Chief Walters finally spoke to her father after he found us hiding in the janitor's closet at the police station. We were crime solving, but he saw it more as crime committing.

Now we headed for home walking slow, neither of us really wanting to get to the bend in the road where we parted. We talked about tomorrow's math quiz and Billy Wallis's mustache, which we both figured had to be his mother's eyebrow pencil on account of it was smeared after gym, and what we wanted to do this summer and what we really would end up doing. Then I blurted out, "They're doing tests on Mama."

Marcy took my hand.

"We don't know anything yet, just that they're doing tests. It's not anything to do with drinking.

And they think maybe my granddaddy was the same. But they're not saying anything more. Just doing tests."

"Well, at least she's not hitting the bottle."

"I wish she *were* drinking. At least they can fix that. What if they can't fix her, Marcy? What if she goes on getting worse? I couldn't even look her in the face after what happened at the market. What will happen to us when she comes home?"

"Maybe you could talk to the monsignor."

"I've been praying my knees raw. I'm scared."

"It must be scary. I try and imagine how you'd be feeling, worrying so about your mama."

"Oh, Marcy, it's Mama I'm scared of and me I'm worried about. Is that awful? I feel wicked, it not being the other way around."

"It's not wicked at all. It's how anyone would feel."

"That's not true. If I were really good, my worries would be for Mama and her getting well. I'm just not good enough. That's why God isn't listening to my prayers." I kicked a stone that had rolled into one of the gulleys. The ruts were worn down and packed hard from the comings and goings of cars along the dirt lane. The stone rolled to a stop in a clump of weeds growing on top of the hump between the gulleys. "I wish things were the way they used to be."

We were quiet then. I guess she figured there wasn't a whole lot she could say. Nothing that would change things. When we came to the place where we parted ways, Marcy said, "Good luck." I must have looked confused, because she added hastily, "On the math quiz tomorrow."

We'd started our separate ways when I heard Marcy running toward me. She nearly ran me over. She threw her arms around me. "Melanie Genzler, you *are* good."

. . .

Walking home I conjured up a picture of Mama the way she was before. I was focusing so hard on keeping her face from twisting the way it did now, I almost missed noticing the flower beds out front. A dozen tulips had been cut from the border. I raced the rest of the way up the drive and tossed my books on the floor of the mudroom, hollering "Mama" loud enough to wake the dead.

Chapter
11

I GUESS I WAS EXPECTING that television commercial. The one in the field of tall grasses and wildflowers. The one where two loved ones come leaping like gazelles from opposite ends of the field, bounding toward each other in slow motion until they are almost touching, then are in the folds of each other's loving arms.

I was playing the slowmotion, sunglowing, gentlyswaying film in my brain so realistically that when I ran into the den, I was swinging my arms in a mock slow-motion kind of way, humping my back and landing on the balls of my my feet in an exaggerated fashion. But when I reached the doorway, the film stuck in a freeze frame and stayed there, tugging and flickering.

It took me near a full minute to realize it wasn't the film in my head that was jumping around. It was Mama in her wheelchair. Her face was jerking and contorting out of time with her hands and feet.

Beside Mama, on the table, in the crystal vase, were the tulips. I looked from Papa to the faces of the church ladies speckling the room.

"That's all wrong. Those go on her dressing table." I couldn't bring myself to call that stranger sitting in the wheelchair Mama. "This is where the lilacs belong."

I took the tulips up to my parents' bedroom, but instead of putting them on her dressing table, I sat on the edge of her bed and stroked the soft petals.

I could hear them talking downstairs in hushed voices. I snuck to the landing and hung over the banister until I could make out what they were saying. I kept hearing the words "Huntington's chorea" . . . "dementia" . . . "hereditary." When they left, I went into my room and got a No. 2 yellow Ticonderoga pencil. I stuck it in the sharpener and started turning the crank. When I finally pulled the pencil out, it was no more than a stub with an eraser on the end.

I carefully printed each of those words in block letters on a single line on a page in my spiral school notebook. I was going to look those words up in the *Encyclopaedia Britannica* when I could get to the library. Right now, though, I was going to take a nap. I was so tired. So very tired.

. . .

I dreamed we were at the lake house. Mama had her easel set up at the end of the dock and was painting the sun rising out of the lake. Papa stood beside her fly fishing, casting with a lazy swing that sent his lure far into the water. The line zinging out sounded like the dentist's drill. Mama'd step back, judging her canvas to see if she'd captured the sunlight's glimmering path to the dock, cocking her head and pursing her lips. In my dream she didn't talk to the painting. She didn't twitch any either. We were like before.

I woke up to Papa sitting on the edge of my

bed. I don't know how long he'd been sitting there, staring down at me. I didn't want to leave my dream. My eyelids fluttered. His voice started from someplace far off soaring in close. "Your mama's taking a nap. The trip tuckered her out."

Papa took me away from my dream. Anger filled me with a blast like the quitting-time steam whistle at the mill. Filled me hot and loud. My ears near burst with the pressure. I fought against my arms as if they had a will of their own. I fought to keep them from striking Papa. I held them pressed tight into my sides for fear they'd fly up on their own accord and smash his face. Beating it, beating it until I was so weary I hadn't the strength to hit him anymore.

But I couldn't hold my tongue. Even my saliva tasted bitter, souring every word. "I got to go to the library. I got a report for school on Huntington's chorea."

He flinched when I said those words, but otherwise there was no telling I'd hurt him. I wanted to hurt him. I wanted him to bellow with the rage I felt. I wanted him to stomp the floorboards and punch in the walls. But he just sat there hunched over on the edge of my bed.

I felt I'd said a blasphemous thing. I pulled the covers around me for protection from the evil-sounding words. Papa's jaw was set in a hard line. He tucked in my bedclothes gently and stood.

He hovered in the doorway a moment. I waited for him to say something, anything. But he didn't say a word, and finally I heard his footsteps fade into his bedroom.

Chapter 12

A FULL MOON LIT THE WAY home. It washed the stores lining Main Street in a silver glow. May Parker's general store, Joe's filling station, and the post office looked all black and silver like Grandma Darling Heart's antique teapot before polishing. Even the flowering quince behind the picket fence in front of Mrs. Barton's boardinghouse gave up its color to the moon.

At the library I'd taken out my list of words. The ones I'd written while eavesdropping on the church ladies. I'd stacked the encyclopedia volumes on the library table in the reference section. Then I'd headed for the card catalogue to see what else there might be.

I was still bent over a half dozen open books

when Miss Kramer, the librarian, put a hand on my shoulder and told me the library was about to close. I looked up, confused, as if I were pulling myself out of a heavy sleep. Most of the overhead lights were turned off. Miss Kramer already had her coat on and her keys in her hand. I stretched like old Sage, feeling the stiffness in my back and neck.

I had found meaning to those strange words listed in my notebook. It brought no comfort. At first I'd taken notes, filling pages and pages of my spiral notebook with a cramped scrawl not even I would be able to decipher later. Soon I realized I wouldn't be needing any notes. I wasn't likely to forget.

As I walked home those words drifted around me. "Huntington's," "chorea," "hereditary." How was I ever to sleep again, knowing those words?

Marcy Davis and I used to take flashlights down to her root cellar and tell stories about vampires and werewolves. We'd sit surrounded by thick cobwebs and years of dust trying to scare the bejeebers out of each other. Invariably some rodent would start scratching on a milk crate in a shadowed corner of the cellar. That would send us shrieking up the cellar stairs, pulling on each other for fear of being the one left behind to be gobbled up by some freak of nature.

How do you run from the real monsters? The monsters that are locked under your skin? Monsters with names like Huntington's?

I had followed the references in the library, going from one clue to the next like a rat caught in a maze. In the end I had a stack on the library table half as tall as I was. The bindings on the heavy volumes creaked when I opened them, the pages crackled when I turned them. I felt distant from all the big words. Just words printed on paper. Fact after fact.

The chorea part was what I'd been seeing, the jerks and twitches, making Mama look like she was being jolted by a live wire. But chorea could also be Sydenham's or Parkinson's. All it meant was involuntary movement—dancelike, the books said. Huntington's chorea was special, really special: You got to go crazy. It worked slow, never stopping, progressive dementia they called it, meaning it eats away at your brain until you are stark raving mad and there's not a thing anyone can do about it.

In the moonlight, on my way home, the words came closer. Smothering me. "Huntington's chorea." "No cure." "Progressive dementia." "Madness." What I couldn't get out of my head, the one article about chorea that wouldn't leave me alone, was the one about St. Vitus' dance, the dance of death, during the Middle Ages. I could picture those people. Picture them convulsing, gripped by the frenzy, in the chapels of St. Vitus. Dancing for the saint who cures. Puppets to a puppeteer gone mad. I could picture them because Mama was hearing their demonic melody. She was dancing the dance of death. St. Vitus' dance.

Chapter
13

I LOOKED BACK DOWN the street toward town before rapping on Miss Rosilda's door. No one was about. The tinkling of the wind chimes hanging on her breezy front porch seemed to call attention to my standing there, like some old neon sign with arrows pointing at me flashing, "Melanie Genzler is seeing a psychic." No one but a barn swallow was there to witness. I knew what had brought me here. But I still couldn't believe I was actually doing it.

Miss Rosilda opened the door before I finished knocking. I barely was able to keep from finishing up on her forehead. Must be convenient to be clairvoyant. Takes the need out of doorbells and such.

Now that I stood here on the threshold of my destiny, I didn't know what to say.

Miss Rosilda cordially invited me in, all the while patting my hand with her own chubby one. Her red hair was twisted and held in place with chopsticks. When she caught me staring at her feet—one clad in a loafer, the other bare—she lifted the shoeless foot up and said, "Sore corn."

"You must know about Mama." I was speaking about Miss Rosilda's special powers.

"There's been speculation around town, but perhaps you should tell me the facts, considering the reliability of the local rumor mill."

I was sure she knew all there was to know, but not wanting to be rude, I told her of Mama's return and the words I'd overheard.

"I looked up every one in the library. Most of it was scientific stuff. But this much I know for a fact. There's no cure."

I was holding back and I knew she knew I was holding back, but I didn't want it appearing foremost on my mind. After all, my first concern should be Mama. Then I remembered Miss Rosilda was psychic and there was no use playing games with her, so I blurted out what was really bothering me. "It's hereditary, you know.

I've got a fifty-fifty chance of getting it too. Same as a coin toss. Will I end up like Mama?"

Clearly Miss Rosilda was flustered. I took this to be a sign. A sign that I was doomed. If I didn't have it, wouldn't she just tell me outright and soothe my fears? I was doomed, I just knew it. I'd be doing St. Vitus' dance just like Mama.

Miss Rosilda put a firm hand on my arm. She turned me to face her and took both my hands in hers. Looking straight into my eyes, she said, "I don't know."

I stood there confused. Did this mean she wasn't sure? Maybe she needed to read my palm or study my tea leaves. Was further testing required?

She must have seen I was ready for whatever was necessary to determine my destiny.

"What makes you think I can see into the future? Oh sure, I may tell May Parker to choose green when redecorating her parlor, that she'll never tire of it. What's so hard about that? The woman dresses in green nearly every day." Miss Rosilda squeezed my hands. "I can't see into the future any better than you can."

"But Mrs. Barton said you told her where to find her great-grandmother's brooch. You led her directly to it." I was sounding desperate now.

"I took Mrs. Barton on a spiritual voyage to where she wore it last." Miss Rosilda laughed, but there was no cheer in it. "It was still pinned to her funeral clothes. Had someone else the courtesy to die before she came to me, she would have found it herself."

"But surely you knew about Mama."

"Anyone with eyesight could see your mama failing."

"But before, when you pushed her out of your house making the sign of the cross?"

"I only knew what your mother really thought of me and was too polite to say. I was getting a little revenge. It was cruel and stupid, but not clairvoyant."

She led me to a chair by the fireplace, where I sat quivering like a cornered rabbit. She sat at my feet, still holding my hands, stroking the backs of them.

"I'm sorry, child."

"What if I have it? What if I start doing St. Vitus' dance?"

She scooted me over and sat with me in the fireside chair. She put her arm around me and rested her chin on top of my head. She started swaying, cooing as though she were calming an infant.

"Oh Miss Rosilda, I just want to curl up and die."

Miss Rosilda kept up her rhythmic rocking, hushing and humming while I wept like a baby on her shoulder.

Later I realized she never once chided me for worrying about only me when it was Mama hope had run out on.

Chapter
14

*W*HEN I GOT HOME from Miss Rosilda's, I found Papa in the den. I leaned against the door-jamb. His desk lamp carpeted the room with a circle of yellow light. I stood outside the golden rim watching Papa shuffle through piles of paper littering his desk. Looked as if he were doing the worksheets Miss Olebar assigned us with tedious regularity. It didn't have the look of normal paperwork from the mill.

I fell into the overstuffed wing chair alongside his desk. The springs were gone in the seat so it poked in odd places, soft here, hard there, but Papa wouldn't hear of getting rid of it. It was his favorite reading chair. Said he had it broken in just right.

I threw my legs over the lumpy stuffed arm and began studying the cuticle on my little finger.

Papa peered out at me over his reading glasses. "I'm quite sure these are in English, yes, quite sure." Papa rubbed his temples in little circles. "How's a body to make sense of this?"

"Make sense of what, Papa?"

He took his reading glasses off and walked around to the front of his old oak monster of a desk. He leaned against the edge and folded his arms across his chest, clutching the sides of his body with his hands.

"Melanie, I've got to place your mother in the rest home in Clewiston."

I couldn't believe what I was hearing. Mama going to one of those places? Why, I'd read all about those insane asylums. They locked patients in chains and fed them stuff that looked like sawdust mixed in mud. Not Mama, not in one of those places. He couldn't mean it.

"You can't put Mama away."

"We haven't got a choice, Melanie. We can't care for her here. She needs constant attention now. She could hurt herself. She could hurt you. I don't know what else to do."

I ran out of the room. I couldn't bear it. Couldn't bear the thought of Mama locked away, forgotten forever, couldn't bear the look on Papa's face. Couldn't bear the thought that this could be me someday. And deep inside, where I kept things pushed down because they weren't fitting, a feeling rose up. I was glad she was going. Glad I wouldn't have to look at her anymore.

I bit my lip with the shame of it and cried out against the terrible person I truly was. Then I tried to bury that feeling as deep as I could, but it kept peeking out to taunt me.

At the top of the stairs I stopped running. I looked at the closed door to Mama's room. I tiptoed to the door and pushed it silently open. Mama was asleep, her long hair unpinned and fanning the pillow. All three cats were curled into her body. Sage had a paw draped protectively across her neck. He looked up when I entered, then nestled back into place when he saw it was just me. Mama's breathing was soft and easy. She was still.

Why can't things be the way they were? She looks the same sleeping. She looks peaceful. I wish I could feel peaceful. Will I ever feel peaceful again? Like a tongue investigating a loose tooth, I poked and prodded my body with my mind looking for signs. *Am I going to end up like Mama? If I so much as drop a fly ball, will I be able to do it without thinking the disease has come over me? There's no escape. No peace.*

I settled into the rocker at the foot of the bed and, along with the cats, went to sleep watching over Mama.

Chapter
15

*P*APA TOOK THE DAY OFF from the mill to get Mama settled into Shady Oaks Farm. They always have names like that. But they weren't fooling me. I knew better. No matter how peaceful the name, I knew her sleep would be forever tormented by the moaning and chain rattling of the insane. I never thought that her own voice would ring louder than the others. I pictured her as before, lost and bewildered in a dank dungeon by the name of Shady Oaks Farm.

When I got home from school, Papa had come back from getting Mama over to the home and was going through her things. Their bed was buried under cardboard boxes from the store-room at May Parker's general store.

He heard me coming up the steps and called to me from their room.

"Melanie, can you give me a hand here? I'm not sure I know what a woman might need."

Papa had all the bureau drawers pulled open and the doors to her side of the walk-in closet swung wide. Dresses lay draped over the rocker, and Papa stood examining her gardening poncho at arm's length.

"You go through the dresser. Pack whatever you think she'll need. What in tarnation is this?"

I hadn't said a word. I pressed my lips together as tight as they would go. Squeezed them into a thin line, determined to do this job without giving him any relief from that horsehair shirt he was wearing. He deserved to be feeling guilty. Deserved it. Why, abandoning Mama in one of those places had to be a mortal sin.

Everything inside the dresser drawers was neatly folded, Mama's things on the left, Papa's on the right, side by side, like a bride and groom at the altar. I'd come to the third drawer down and was lifting a stack of Mama's starched white blouses when I noticed pink tissue paper sticking out from under Papa's Sunday shirts.

I looked over my shoulder to where Papa was holding bottles of liquid up to the light, sniffing at their stoppers and scratching his head. I guess he decided just to bring them all, because he started wrapping them in yesterday's newspaper.

I put my body between the dresser drawer and where he stood packing. Taking the tissue-paper bundle from its hiding place, I unwrapped it.

Hidden in the crinkly folds of the pink tissue was the lumpy plaster of paris bowl I'd shaped in kindergarten as an ashtray for Papa. The paint was faded and the plaster crumbly. I'd thought he'd thrown it out when he quit smoking years ago.

I remembered that Christmas morning. I had paused in my frenzied unwrapping long enough to direct Papa in the opening of his gift. The gift I'd labored over under the stern eye of my kindergarten teacher, Miss Morgan. I informed him proudly that it was an ashtray, to clear the air of any confusion as to its purpose. Miss Morgan had insisted on candy dishes. I would have none of it. It was my first act of rebellion, and I was determined to win.

He'd held it aloft, turning it this way and

that, as though it were as precious as the Hope diamond, and every night until the day he quit smoking he made a big hullaballoo about pulling out his favorite ashtray or things wouldn't be quite right.

He'd saved it. Saved it all these years. Saved this crumbly lump of plaster I'd made just for him.

Papa came up behind me. He smiled that big old lopsided grin of his and, nodding at the ashtray, said, "Knew things would never be quite right if I didn't have my favorite ashtray."

Forgetting all about my tight-lipped vow, I blurted out at him, "Well, things aren't quite right now, are they?"

Even though he never moved a single muscle, the smile in his face drained away like water when someone pulls the plug on the bathtub, leaving it empty.

I shoved the ashtray against his chest and started packing with fury. Papa sat down on the edge of the bed holding the ashtray.

I flung open drawers and tossed their contents over my shoulder in the general direction of the boxes, creating a blizzard of undergarments.

Papa ignored me. He sat looking at the ash-tray he held in his hands, tears welling in his eyes. Then gently he wrapped the worn tissue paper around it and put it back under his best shirts.

My anger spent, I wanted to fall into his arms and weep. But I didn't know how to put an end to the mess I'd begun. So carefully now, almost reverently, I packed the boxes with all that was dear to Mama, to be taken to Shady Oaks Farm.

I helped Papa cart out the last of the boxes, hoisting them onto the tailgate and pushing them down the bed of the truck. When we'd finished, he opened the passenger door for me.

"I'm not going," I said.

He looked at me closely, chewing the inside of his cheek. He must have known by the tone of my voice I meant business, because he didn't put up a fight. I'd read about those places. I wasn't about to set foot in one.

Chapter
16

ONE EVENING WHILE PAPA was at the rest home visiting Mama, I took up a *Good Housekeeping* magazine of Mama's and leafed through it. At first I was just flipping pages because I couldn't think of anything else to do and I was afraid to be alone with my thoughts these days. Then a picture of a casserole set my mouth to watering.

The recipe claimed even the most inexperienced cook couldn't fail. Figuring there couldn't be many with less experience at cooking than me, I cut out the recipe. I stuck it to the refrigerator door with one of the magnets Mama used for displaying my school papers before I told her it was embarrassing. I was much too old to have things pinned up for my friends to see when they came over. She still had the magnets but used them for her lists now. Or at least before.

I figured I'd look at the recipe for a few days, then maybe try it. The picture sure was pretty, even had a sprig of greens for garnishing. Maybe Mama's herb garden would have a sprig like the one in the picture. I was not so inexperienced as to think that my creation would look anything like the picture in the magazine. Still, I was willing to give it a try.

When Papa came home from the mill that Wednesday in May, I was in Mama's butchering apron sautéing onions. I'd looked up *sauté* in the dictionary, since the recipe called for me to do it. All it meant was frying, which I'd witnessed Mama do a hundred times. Sautéing sounded much more complicated, so when Papa sniffed the air and asked what I was up to, I said, "Why, I'm sautéing onions, Papa."

"Sure does smell fine." He went to the cupboard, collecting plates to set the table. "I had to let Howie Jenkins go today," he said above the clatter. He tried to say it matter-of-fact, like he was talking about the weather, but he wasn't fooling me. I knew how he felt about everyone at the mill. Especially Mr. Jenkins.

"Papa, he's been with you forever."

"The orders have fallen off by nearly a third. It's a struggle to meet payroll. I'm going to take on Howie's job till things pick up; then we can bring him back in."

"What did he say when you told him?"

"He knew it was coming. He knows if there was any other way . . . but with Lil, and the cost at Shady Oaks . . ."

I stirred the onions and added the garlic. The smell filled the kitchen.

"You won't lose the mill, will you, Papa?" I was afraid to look at him for fear he might say yes.

"Oh no, nothing like that. Our medical insurance is picking up most of it. The rest—well, I figure I might sell the lake house."

"Oh Papa, not the lake house. That was to be your and Mama's retirement home."

"Well, I don't think I'll be spending much time there." Papa folded the napkins and slipped them under the forks.

I tried to imagine the lake house without

Mama, without her humming in the kitchen, without her reading in the porch hammock, without her rowing in circles just beyond the dock on account of she was too scared to go to the middle, rumor being it was a bottomless lake. Papa was right.

I smelled something burning, but by the time it registered that I was the one cooking here, clouds of smoke hovered near the ceiling. I pulled the frying pan off the burner. The bottom of the pan was black. Curses, that would be impossible to get off. The onions were all stuck to the pan.

"I don't think we can salvage this," I said, looking into the charred remains of the foolproof recipe.

"Can we do something with this?" Papa asked, pointing to the rest of the ingredients lined up on the counter.

We stood staring, neither of us knowing where to begin, when the doorbell rang. We both just looked at each other. No one had come to call since folks had discovered Mama was suffering from Huntington's. Guess they were afraid it was catching or something. It sounds silly to say that we had forgotten what that ringing might mean. It must have been we just weren't expecting anyone.

The doorbell chimed again.

Papa moved first, swinging the door wide. "Why, Miss Lamour, how nice of you to call."

Miss Rosilda? Here?

"Won't you come in?" Papa asked her, waving the smoke out the front door. "We've had a small accident with sauté."

Miss Rosilda held out a covered casserole with potholders. "I brought you something for supper."

"You must be psychic. We just destroyed our dinner." Papa realized then what he had said. The red started rising in his face like the thermometer on a hot day.

"Well now, Mr. Genzler, that's what they say." She winked at Papa.

"It's George," Papa said with that grin of his. "Won't you join us?" And before she could answer, Papa had another plate on the table and was going for the silver.

Chapter
17

$\mathscr{P}$APA DROVE THE HOUR to Clewiston every
Tuesday and Thursday after supper and spent
nearly all day Sunday with Mama at Shady Oaks.

He never asked me to come along on week-
nights, not wanting me to get behind on my
schoolwork, but every Sunday he'd stand crum-
pling up the brim of his hat and ask if I'd like to
come.

"One of us should be going to church and
praying for her recovery," I said, even though I
hadn't set foot inside our church since the day
Papa drove Mama off to that place.

"She's not going to be getting better,
Melanie."

I ran from the room, my hands clamped over

my ears, singing the national anthem at the top of my lungs.

Papa never argued, just rode off in the truck. He never talked about how she was when he got home, and I never asked.

On the evenings Papa stayed home, after supper we'd do up dishes together. I'd wash and he'd dry. One night we got to jawing about the literature course I was taking. Next thing I knew, I was reading to Papa. Before long it became our nightly ritual. Papa'd pull the footrest up to his favorite chair while I took out my assignment. I'd slump down into his desk chair, put my feet up on the old oak desk, and read out loud. Even the cats came into the den to curl up and listen.

My teacher was hard pressed keeping me in reading material that spring. Most nights I'd read until I was hoarse. Papa'd be sitting back with his eyes closed, but if I stopped to check and see if he'd dozed off, his head would come popping up to see what was keeping me.

His favorite book that spring was *The Old Man and the Sea*. At first I thought he took a liking to it because of the fishing. I came to think otherwise.

"Why doesn't he just cut the line?" I asked one night, exasperated by Santiago's persistence over a fool fish. "Doesn't he see it's hopeless?"

"Fishing is all he knows. It's what he is," Papa said, just like the old man was one of his good friends.

I realized then it wasn't the fishing that captured Papa; it was Santiago's battle. A battle Santiago knew he'd not be winning, knew it from the start. But it made no difference. He'd fight it just the same.

. . .

We never talked of Mama. The only time we even mentioned her name was Sundays, when Papa asked if I'd be going to see her. And then he was the only one who actually said her name.

I stopped lying about going to church or having homework. I just said no these days and walked into the house after his truck disappeared down the lane in a cloud of dust. The cats all turned their backs on me and walked away, their tails aloft, swishing angrily.

Chapter
18

THE TOWNSFOLK TOOK to crossing the street when they'd see me coming. Scurrying away, eyes glued to the pavement. I'd keep my head up high and my eyes forward, but out of the corner of my eye I could see them huddling in my wake, most shaking their heads in Christian piety but not all. No, I saw those who laughed.

I'd pass the windows of May Parker's general store and see them laughing. Oh, they'd pretend not to see me coming, their backs to the window, but I knew what they were laughing at. I knew it.

The worst of it was the church ladies. With their flapping jowls. Stopping me on my way to school asking after Mama. Asking as if they really cared. All they really cared about was bragging at their ladies' auxiliary meetings how they were beyond reproach; after all, they had performed their moral duty. So now they could feel holy and charitable in their Christian souls. Clucking among themselves when their hands were still able to control the knitting needles that shaped the caps for the poor and needy. *They better not show up with a basket at our door. No telling what I would do if they should do such a thing. I know what I'd like to do. Take their basket and cram it over their fat heads.*

I could stand the kids at school ignoring me. Most didn't know what to say, so they just pretended I wasn't there. I figured I had a good idea as to how the invisible man must have felt. Marcy took to walking me to my classes, keeping up a constant chatter as if talking twice as much would make up for everyone else's silence. Marcy couldn't understand I didn't mind being ignored. For her that would be the worst. But I could stand that.

It was in the cafeteria that the wild thing came over me. The Bigelow twins were in the far corner by the trash can. Kids were lined up waiting their turn to empty their lunch trays and get to class. Erica Bigelow was entertaining the line with a performance. She was flailing her arms and making strange sounds. Something inside me broke loose.

I tucked my head down and charged. I hurtled across the cafeteria gaining speed and aiming my head like a battering ram for Erica's gut. When I hit her, my momentum took us crashing up against the wall. I could hear the air leave Erica with a grunt. I set my arms to pinwheeling, but with my eyes squeezed shut, my pummeling fists connected with parts of Erica only half the time. The rest of the time they hit the wall, hurting like the very devil.

Hands, dozens of them, were grabbing at me, hauling me off of Erica Bigelow. Someone had me around the waist, someone had each arm, and others had hold of my legs. I still was blindly hitting, although now I was dragging the weight of half a dozen of my classmates so my punches were like hitting under water. But I didn't stop.

I could hear Marcy calling out my name. "Melanie, Melanie, Melanie, she wasn't doing your mama, it was Miss Olebar, she was telling about Miss Olebar and the mud wasps, Melanie. She wasn't doing your mama."

I collapsed in a heap, the others parting like the Red Sea for Mr. Forsyth, our principal. He grabbed hold of my arm and pulled me up to my feet, but I couldn't get my legs to support me, so he dragged me to the nearest chair and set me in it.

"Everyone stay right where you are," he bellowed. When he'd extracted what he needed from those standing around, he told them to get to their classes. I started to pull myself to my feet. "Except for you, young lady. You're coming with me."

Mr. Forsyth set Miss O'Brien, the secretary, to the task of getting hold of Papa and left me on the bench outside his office. I sat there biting my lip to keep from crying. The longer he had me sitting there, the less I felt like crying. I'd made a fool of myself. Jaws'd be wagging on that for sure. But I didn't care anymore. Let them talk. I didn't give a rat's turd.

Mr. Forsyth opened his office door. He held the switch in one hand.

"Fighting is a very serious offense. I am going to suspend you for three days. In addition, you shall feel the bite of the lash for your crime. Miss O'Brien, if you'd kindly come in to stand witness to the switching."

I heard the whistle of the switch and tensed for the sting on my bare calf. It stung worse than a bee. A long narrow welt came up right away. Angry red. Mr. Forsyth didn't switch fast and get it over. He liked to lecture between strokes, or so I'd heard tell. I'd never been in trouble before, so I couldn't say firsthand.

"Fighting is not allowed in this school."

I heard the whistle again, my body cringing, knowing what to expect this time. But nothing came. I opened my eyes and saw Papa standing there. He had Mr. Forsyth's wrist in a grip that was turning his knuckles white with the force.

"You'll not be touching my daughter, I don't believe."

Mr. Forsyth was sputtering spit, he was so mad. "Mr. Genzler, your interference here amounts to sparing the rod and spoiling this child."

Papa held on to Mr. Forsyth's wrist, and by the

way he was twisting it, I would venture it was causing Mr. Forsyth more than a little discomfort. "You touch her again, Mr. Forsyth, and I'll see to it that you are without employment. Times are hard, Mr. Forsyth, so I'd think carefully."

"See here, this child was fighting on school grounds. Just because you own the mill doesn't give you any right . . ."

I knew Papa was powerful, owning the mill and all. The town's sole industry. But I'd never seen him use that power. He loved his work, and most times at the mill a stranger looking on would never be able to tell who was the boss. He was that way. So it came as quite a surprise to me that Mr. Forsyth would be acting so nervous.

Papa let go of his wrist then and straightened Mr. Forsyth's lapels for him, brushing away some lint but never taking his eyes away from Mr. Forsyth's.

"I'll be taking her home now, but tomorrow morning she'll be coming back. I'll be very interested in how her day went when she gets home. Do we understand each other, Mr. Forsyth?"

"Well, I guess we could take into consideration the emotional strain your family is under at present."

"That's very considerate," Papa said.

. . .

In the truck on the way home I started blubbering. All the tears I'd fought shedding, sitting on the bench outside Mr. Forsyth's office, came pouring out of me now. Papa took one hand off the wheel and pulled me over to him. I buried my face in his shoulder. As he drove over the bumpy road, my head bounced on his shoulder. I was soaking the sleeve of his new oxford shirt with my leaking.

"It's all my fault," I said, getting the words out in a fit of stops and starts.

"What's all your fault?" Papa asked me, using his knee and one hand to turn onto Dunn's Lane.

"Don't you see, I wished someone would come take her away, I even wished she was dead, and now she's gone and she's dying." My confession left me feeling empty.

"She is dying. Wishing with all your heart and soul won't change that. I know."

"I wish things were like they were. I wish things didn't change."

"I know, honey. Me too."

"The worst of it is, all I can think about is what if I get it? I should be feeling sad for her, but instead all I can think about is me turning into . . ." I didn't know how to put it so it wouldn't hurt Papa. That thing? That monster? It wasn't Mama anymore. Not to me.

"If anyone's to blame here, it's me." Papa slowed the truck. "We should have talked long before this. I've been caught up with my own problems. I should have been helping you see to yours."

I couldn't believe Papa was feeling guilty, too. "What would Mama have said right now?"

"I think she would say it was high time we stopped worrying on what we should be feeling and take care of what we *are* feeling."

I nodded. I could almost hear her say it.

We rattled up our drive. Papa stopped the truck and we just sat there. I wasn't crying anymore, but my head was still on his shoulder and I was watching the sky out the windshield. The sun had a red cast to it. Grandma Darling Heart always said a red sun has water in its eye.

Chapter
19

I GOT UP EARLY SUNDAY morning. Before Papa. I took the shoebox down from the top shelf in my closet. I put on my best dress and sat on the deacon's bench waiting on Papa. Flashing those patent leather shoes.

It was the first time since Mama left that I'd seen a smile that brought the light into his eyes.

"Well now, this calls for a celebration. What say we stop at the International House of Pancakes in Clewiston for breakfast?"

"Can I have blueberry syrup?" I asked, hooking my arm in his.

The air was dry and the sky bluer than I'd seen it yet this spring. We rode the whole way to Clewiston with the windows all the way down and the radio blaring. I rested my arm on the truck door and hung my head out the window. I had to close my eyes because the wind kept snapping my hair across my eyes and into my mouth.

I should have felt good except my stomach was percolating. I was preparing myself for the dirt and the screams and the smells. I was sure I'd probably faint from the wailing sounds. I could already hear them echoing around the dungeonlike corridors of the asylum, and we hadn't even entered the city limits yet.

After breakfast I was confused when Papa stopped the truck outside a great big rambling colonial house. Were we visiting someone here in Clewiston besides Mama? I'd never heard talk of anyone we knew personally in town.

Papa came around and held open the truck door for me. "Here we are."

I looked up, checking windows for bodies plastered against the glass desperate for escape. The curtains tied back at each window revealed nothing, hid nothing. One window was open. There weren't even bars on it.

Papa held open the front door for me, and I

stepped into a large foyer. A massive staircase rose directly in front of me. Beside the staircase and tucked under it just a bit was a desk like a receptionist's desk in a hotel. A woman in a crisp white uniform and nurse's cap sat writing in a notebook.

"Why Mr. Genzler, how nice to see you, and who have we here?"

"This is my daughter, Melanie."

"Mrs. Genzler will be so happy to see you, dear. I believe she is in the drawing room right now."

The arched entrance to the drawing room was across from the nurse's station. I stood rooted to the spot. Classical music floated out of the room. No screams, no wailings. The room was wallpapered in blue fleurs-de-lis. The fringe of a large oriental carpet was visible from where I stood. I couldn't see very far into the room. I couldn't see anyone.

Papa took my arm and drew me toward the room. My feet didn't want to follow. I dragged them, but Papa didn't seem to notice. He seemed eager to get to Mama. How could he be eager?

She looked old. Slumped in the wheelchair. They'd even thrown a shawl over her shoulders. Like Grandma Darling Heart wore, certainly not Mama. I took it off her shoulders when I leaned over to kiss her and spread it across her lap. Papa kissed her too, and we pulled chairs directly in front of her.

"She's on a medication to control the movements so she won't hurt herself," Papa said to me, holding Mama's hands in both of his. "But I'm convinced she knows."

"Georgie, who's your lady friend?" a woman asked Papa from across the room.

"Why Mabel, you are looking lovely today. This is my daughter, Melanie. Melanie, I'd like you to meet Mama's charming roommate, Mrs. McGee."

Mrs. McGee looked to be one hundred fifty years old. She looked dry and brittle, as if she'd collapse in a pile of ash. But she grabbed her walker, lifting it high, and scooted over to us, never once putting it down for support. Papa fetched another chair for Mrs. McGee.

"They make me use this blasted thing," she said, banging it on the floor. "Afraid I'll fall. Poppycock."

Mrs. McGee put her bony fingers on my arm, clamping hard. It felt like old chicken bones. "Child, you are the image of your mother."

Papa could see I was uneasy. "Mrs. McGee, where's that fine gentleman friend of yours?"

Mrs. McGee and Papa talked back and forth about Mama. They talked about how she slept and what she ate. Sounded like Mama was doing better than Papa and me, at least dietarily. Mama dozed in the chair. She'd nod off, then bring her head up sharply. When she was awake, she seemed interested in the conversation. I think Papa was right. I think she did know we were there. Maybe something of Mama was in there.

I was amazed at how lovely the house was. The nurses and orderlies were cheerful and friendly, joking with everyone while making sure they were comfortable. Mama still smelled of rose petals and witch hazel. If I closed my eyes and breathed deep, I could smell her familiar smell. I let the music float all over my body, and I was almost calm.

On our way out of the house I'd stuffed the paperback I'd been reading to Papa into my sweater pocket, thinking if the truck ride got boring, I could read a spell. The book slipped out of my pocket and fell onto the carpet.

Papa picked it up, handed it to me, and asked, "Why don't you read to us all?"

He settled into his chair, sure I'd say yes, never having denied him before. Mrs. McGee copied Papa, lifting her legs onto a footstool first, then clasping her hands in her lap and closing her eyes. How could I say no after such preparations?

We'd been reading *The Pearl* by John Steinbeck and had left off where the baby had been bitten by a scorpion. I found the page with the corner turned down and started reading, clearing my throat and speaking louder than usual on account of Mrs. McGee being hard of hearing. When I got to the part where Juana, the baby's mama, starts regulating her wanting, not too much, not too little, fearing too much wanting will bring her bad luck, too little won't be strong enough to fix the baby, I knew exactly what she was feeling. It was like when I was saying the Rosary, it had to be just right or it wouldn't work. Mrs. McGee started snoring, a trickle of spittle working its way down her chin, but Mama was wide-awake and watching me with watery eyes.

I was surprised when it was time to head back to Cutter's Falls. Surprised that the time had gone so fast. They let us take Mama to her room. Papa wheeled her, backing her in and setting the brake on the chair. On the table by her bed stood a crystal vase filled with flowers.

Papa saw what I was looking at and said, "The nurses see to it that the vase is kept full."

I kissed Mama good-bye, holding her hands. I could have sworn I felt her squeeze my fingers when I whispered, "I love you."

Chapter
20

WE KNEW IT WAS COMING. With each visit we saw her inching closer to God. She'd stopped eating some time before because swallowing was too hard. Still, when the call came that she had passed on, we couldn't make ourselves believe it. We both thought we'd drive up to Shady Oaks and she'd be waiting for us in the drawing room like always.

Mr. Forsyth himself came to my classroom to fetch me. He whispered something to Miss Olebar, and the way they both looked at me, I knew. Marcy saw it too. She leaped out of her seat and gave me a fierce hug. I didn't want to let go of Marcy, but Mr. Forsyth cleared his throat, and when that failed, Miss Olebar gently pried us apart. No one in the classroom made a sound. I think they all were holding their breaths, it was so quiet.

Papa was waiting in the office for me and wrapped me in his arms when I stepped over the threshold. We walked to the truck not knowing who was holding up who but neither of us cried or said much.

Bumping down Dunn's Lane in the pickup, I said, "I wish she could have seen her roses this year. There's never been so many. Why, they're so thick the weight of the blossoms makes the stems weep."

Papa said, "I think I know just the thing."

When we got home, he got the stepladder from the garage and set it up next to the latticework. Then he put on his heavy gardening gloves and handed me a pair. Climbing the ladder, brandishing pruning shears, he hollered, "Melanie, you get everything you can lay your hands on that holds water."

I ran back and forth from the house with buckets, all Mama's pots and pans, every vase we owned. I filled pickle jars and honey pots with water from the spigot alongside the chimney.

Even the bean pot held the roses Papa kept dropping from the climbing bushes. The back of the pickup was nearly full, a bed of pale-pink petals, soft and heavenly. I was running out of vessels that would hold water. Desperate, I took the cats' water dishes, promising them I'd leave a plugged-up sink full in case they got thirsty before I could return their dishes. Still there were a few stems left. Papa scratched his head. Then a slow grin grew over his face.

"Go fetch my green rubber boots, Melanie."

We filled Papa's boots with the last of the roses. There being no room in the back of the truck, we took them up front in the cab with us and went to see to Mama's coming home.

· · ·

Old Sage died shortly after Mama. Papa and I buried the orange tom under the lilac tree. We surrendered to the earth more than our share that summer; in return, the earth gave us gardens that were truly miraculous. Mama's flowers crowded every corner of the yard, perfuming the air and pillowing the ground.

We'd begun our summer reading list, moving our sessions out onto the porch, where we could breathe the scented air. Some nights we'd spend poring over Mama's gardening books, serenaded by crickets and wood frogs. Weekends we'd apply what we'd learned to the flowerbeds.

There were times working in the gardens I'd sit back on my heels and look over at Papa on his hands and knees working the soil, Bailey helping him dig and Scribbles perched on Papa's flat back squinting in the sun's warmth. Suddenly it would come to me I'd gone nearly half a day without dwelling on my becoming afflicted. What a wonder it was to go so long without fretting. One day I might make it through an entire day without thinking the words "Huntington's chorea." One day I might be able to drop a spoon and just pick it up without thinking a thing of it, the way normal folks do. One day I might go dancing without thinking of St. Vitus. Today I planted a rose garden with Papa.

Author's Note

Huntington's chorea, now generally known as Huntington's disease (HD), is a severe degenerative disorder of the nervous system. The onset of symptoms is most often, although not always, in middle life. In the early stages HD is frequently mistaken for other diseases, notably alcoholism and psychiatric disorders. Initial symptoms may include chorea (involuntary dancelike movements), clumsiness, slurred speech, mood swings, and memory loss.

HD progresses unrelentingly. Dr. George Huntington, who first reported the disease more than 100 years ago, described it as "coming on gradually, but surely, increasing in degrees, and often occupying years in its development, until the hapless sufferer is but a quivering wreck of his former self."

HD is a genetic disorder caused by an error in the person's DNA. The children of a parent with the HD gene have a 50 percent chance of inheriting the disease. There is no "carrier" state.

With the identification of the HD gene in 1993 came the ability to test at-risk individuals with a high degree of certainty. The decision to test or not to test is a difficult one. Should the test prove diagnostic for HD, no cure is available. For those who choose not to test, and for those who find they have the HD gene, life becomes a vigil for the symptoms indicating that they, too, are suffering the fate they may have witnessed unfolding before them.

Advances in genetic research have given birth to bold new ideas regarding the cause of HD. Advances in clinical research have given direction to finding new drugs to halt the progress of HD. The likelihood that effective methods of prevention and therapy will be developed in the near future becomes greater with each new discovery. One day HD will be a horror in memory only, a disease of our past.